Brown Like Me

WRITTEN BY ANDREA CAINE
ILLUSTRATED BY ZACHARY BROWN

MYND
MATTERS

Mynd Matters Publishing
715 Peachtree Street NE
Suites 100 & 200
Atlanta, GA 30308
www.myndmatterspublishing.com

ISBN: 978-1-953307-36-1 (hcv)
ISBN: 978-1-953307-35-4 (pbk)

FIRST EDITION

For Erin,
May you never question the magic
you possess, inside and out.

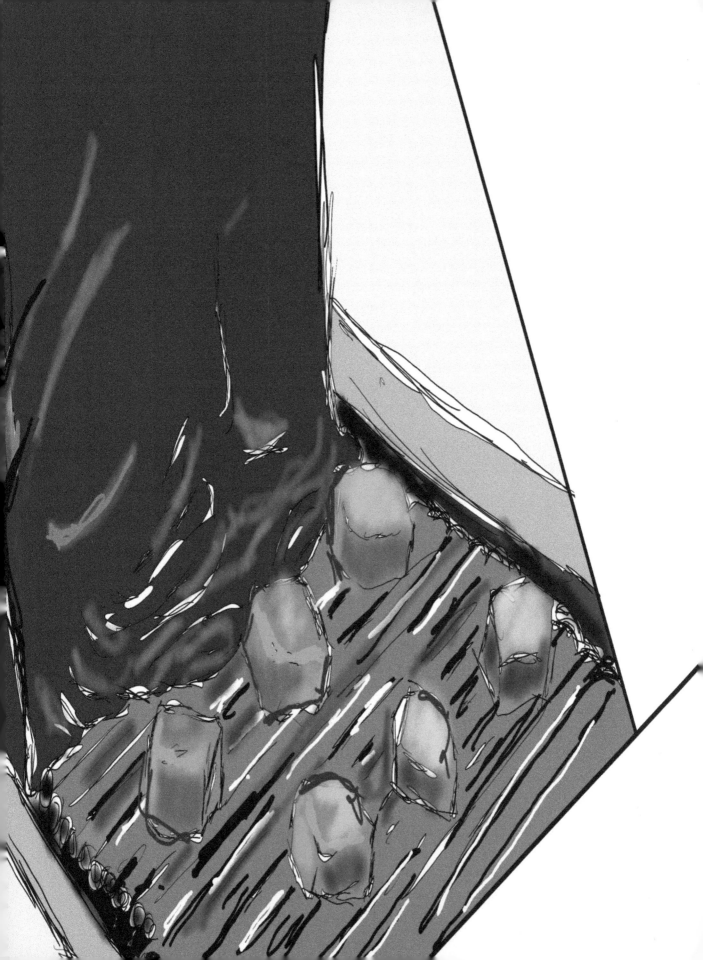

There are so many things that are brown
like me, brown like me, brown like me!
There are so many things that are brown like me.
If you just stop and look, you will see.

I am brown like chocolate, smooth and sweet, with
texture and flavor that runs so deep.
I am brown like caramel, your everyday treat.
There are many things that are brown like me.

There are so many things that are brown
like me, brown like me, brown like me!
There are so many things that are brown like me.
If you just stop and look, you will see.

I am brown like a bear with long, fluffy hair.
So snuggly and warm in the winter.

I am brown like the bear that you cuddle and
share with a brother or cute little sister.

There are so many things that are brown like me,
brown like me, brown like me!
There are so many things that are brown like me.
If you just stop and look, you will see.

I am brown like the bark on a beautiful tree, bearing fruit for everyone to eat. Growing tall from the ground, with my roots reaching down, giving shade from your head to your feet.

There are so many things that are brown like me, brown like me, brown like me!
There are so many things that are brown like me. If you just stop and look, you will see.

I am brown like the clay you mold in your hands.
You can call me a masterpiece.

I am brown like the beach when you play in the sand, bringing you closer toward the sea.

There are so many things that are brown like me, brown like me, brown like me!
There are so many things that are brown like me. If you just stop and look, you will see.

I am brown like a bird, with my wings stretching wide, as I take off into the sky.
Singing sweet little songs, not a thing can go wrong, when I am soaring up so high.

There are so many things that are brown like me, brown like me, brown like me!
There are so many things that are brown like me. If you just stop and look, you will see.

I am brown like the spices you use in your food, bringing flavor to all you taste. Cinnamon, ginger root, vanilla bean. Can't you see what my brown color makes?

There are so many things that are brown like me, brown like me, brown like me!
There are so many things that are brown like me.
If you just stop and look, you will see.

I am brown like my mother and my father, too.
I am brown like cousins, nieces, nephews.

I am brown just like Martin, and Malcolm, and Rosa.
I am brown one hundred, no, one thousand times over!

I am so brown, I wish to be no other color.
So brown in my brownness for my great,
great grandmother.

I am brown in the day and brown in the night.
People look at me and say, "Out of sight!"

There are so many things that are brown like me,
brown like me, brown like me!
There are so many things that are brown like me.
If you just stop and look, you will see.

I am brown like your hair.
I am brown like your eyes.
Take a look in the mirror and be mesmerized.

We're the same, you and I. We both have some brown.
You can see all the brown, if you just look around.

There are so many things that are brown like me,
brown like me, brown like me!
There are so many things that are brown like me.
If you just stop and look, you will see.

B is for beauty, brave, and bodacious.
R is for radiant, respected, resilient.
O is for outstanding, optimist, one of a kind.
W is for wisdom when I am blowing your mind.
N is for nourishment, to make you feel good.

There is brown on my skin and brown in my blood.
I share all my brown with you on this day
So everyone knows there is a way,
To appreciate brown just like all other colors.
We are as equally wonderful as one another.
So, when drawing the picture of the life you see,
Pick up the brown crayon. It is brown like ME!

CPSIA information can be obtained
at www.ICGtesting.com
Printed in the USA
LVHW070351130121
676184LV00019B/712

9 781953 30736